ISAAC AND HIS AMAZING ASPERGER SUPERPOWERS!

melanie walsh

WALKER BOOKS
AND SUBSIDIARIES

LONDON · BOSTON · SYDNEY · AUCKLAND

My name is Isaac and I'm a superhero!

You might think I look just like everyone else, but I've got special superpowers that make me slightly different to my brother and the other kids at school. However some children don't understand this and call me names.

My superhero brain is fantastic and remembers loads of things. I love to tell people interesting facts I know,

cat
rocke
snake

600

but sometimes they just walk away!

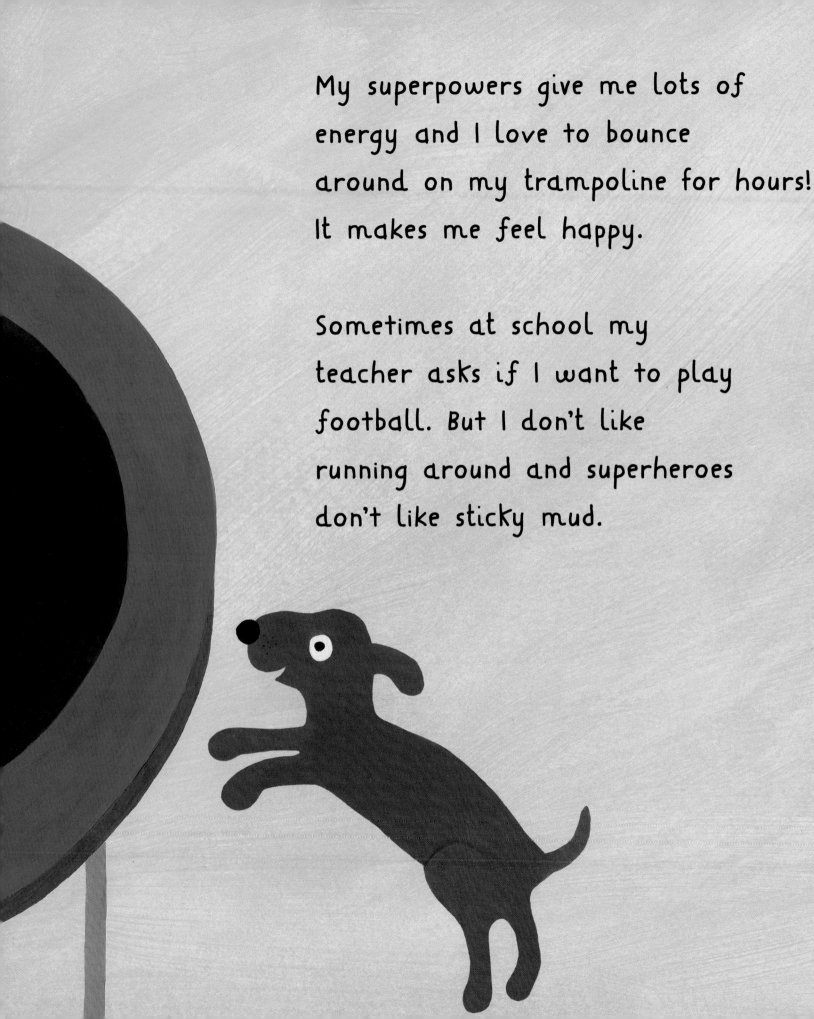

My superpowers give me lots of energy and I love to bounce around on my trampoline for hours! It makes me feel happy.

Sometimes at school my teacher asks if I want to play football. But I don't like running around and superheroes don't like sticky mud.

Oh ... hello.

Because I'm a superhero
I have lots of things
to think about.
I try to remember
to say hello to
people I know, but
sometimes I forget.
I'm not being rude.

My pets understand me and my
superpowers and I love them.
I find it easy to talk to them
and they always listen.

Because my teacher knows I'm a superhero she lets me fidget with my special toy in class. It helps me feel calm and I can listen better.

"Meow," said the little cat.
"Shh," said Mummy.

Shh!

As a superhero I like to tell people what they look like, as they might not know!

My mum says that I should try and keep these thoughts in my head as I might upset people.

Superheroes listen carefully, but sometimes get confused. When my brother told me that my tummy would go POP if I ate too much ...

POP!

I believed him!
I don't really get
jokes like this.

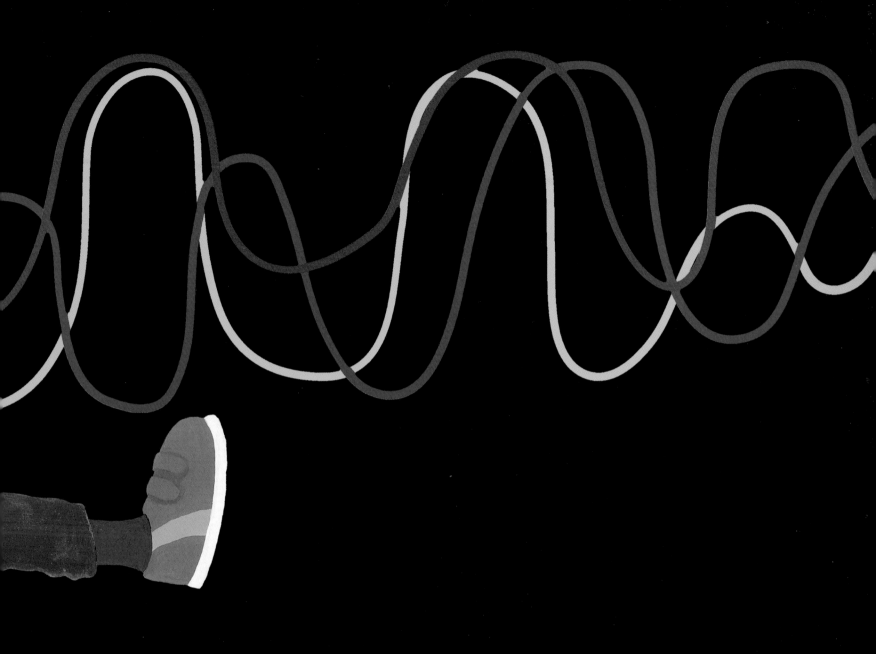

My ears can hear super well.
I can even hear the buzzing
that some lights make in
shops. This makes my ears
really hurt and I feel upset.

I feel scared
when I look people
in the eyes.

My dad taught me a good
superhero trick. I just look
at people's foreheads instead.
It really works!

Superheroes are really good at spotting things.
At playtime if there isn't a game I want to play
I like to use my super-vision to find interesting
things that other people haven't seen!

You may not have guessed, but I'm not really a superhero. I have Asperger's (it rhymes with hamburgers) which is a kind of autism.

You can't catch it. It just means my brain works a little differently.

But I do love
playing superheroes
with my brother.
He understands
me and now
you do too!

If you want to find out more
about topics discussed in this book,
here are some useful links.

Autism and Asperger's Syndrome

National Autistic Society
www.autism.org.uk

Ambitious About Autism
www.ambitiousaboutautism.org.uk

Research Autism
www.researchautism.net

Autism Research Centre
www.autismresearchcentre.com

Autism NI
www.autismni.org

Scottish Autism
www.scottishautism.org

Autism Awareness
www.autismawareness.com.au

Other useful contacts

I Can
www.ican.org.uk

Young Minds
www.youngminds.org.uk

Other books by Melanie Walsh:

ISBN 978-1-4063-4176-8

ISBN 978-1-4063-5995-4

ISBN 978-1-4063-2029-9

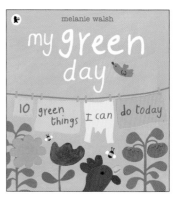

ISBN 978-1-4063-7714-9

Available from all good booksellers

www.walker.co.uk